IN THE GHOST DETECTIVE UNIVERSE:

NOVELS
(Best to be read in order)
Beyond the Grave
Unveiling the Past
Beneath the Surface
Piercing the Veil

SHORT STORIES
(All stand-alone)
Just Desserts
Lost Friends
Family Bonds
Common Ground
Till Death
Family History
Heritage
New Beginnings
Far From Home
Severed Ties
Eternal Bond
Harsh Expectations
Dull Expectations

SHORT STORY COLLECTIONS
Unfinished Business, Vol 1

R.W. WALLACE

Author of *Beyond the Grave*

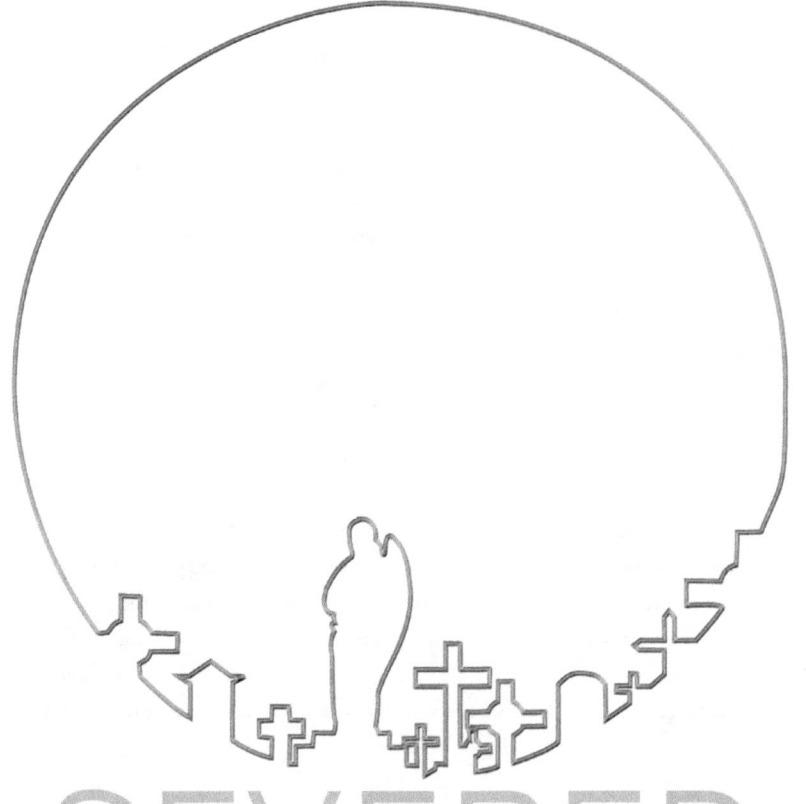

SEVERED TIES

A Ghost Detective Short Story

Severed Ties
by R.W. Wallace

Copyright © 2021 by R.W. Wallace

Cover by R.W. Wallace
Cover Illustration 10926765 © germanjames | 123rf.com
Cover Illustration 193487176 © Bubbers | Depositphotos
Cover Illustration 263199440 © Nouman | Adobe Stock

This story was first published in *Pulphouse Fiction Magazine*, Issue #15

All characters and events in this book, other than those clearly in the public domain, are fictitious and any resemblance to real persons, living or dead, is purely coincidental.

All rights reserved. No part of this publication may be reproduced, distributed, or transmitted in any form or by any means, including photocopying, recording, or other electronic or mechanical methods, without the prior written permission of the publisher, except in the case of brief quotations embodied in critical reviews and certain other noncommercial uses permitted by copyright law. For permission requests, write to the publisher at the address below.

www.rwwallace.com

ISBN paperback: [979-10-95707-93-6]
ISBN ebook: [979-10-95707-94-3]

First edition

ONE

Christmas is a weird time of the year. It can be the most wonderful and heartwarming days of a person's life, just like it can be the absolute worst. There's no in-between. I think the comparison with the perfect days is the reason the bad ones become so bad.

Being ghosts in a cemetery doesn't really change the phenomenon. Except maybe tip the scales away from the cheer and joy.

Now, don't get me wrong. We're not miserable ghosts by any stretch of the imagination. No moaning, very little spooking visitors, no screaming vengeance at the moon. Clothilde tried that last one at one point in the late nineties but couldn't stay serious for long enough to pull it off.

Clothilde and I have celebrated Christmas together more times than either of us did with our respective families when we were alive, and we've developed our own traditions. A couple of times they were adapted because we had a visiting ghost who hadn't resolved their unfinished business yet, but mostly, it's stayed the same through the years.

It starts with the decoration of the church and the manger. We're lucky enough to live in a cemetery belonging to a church where they put the manger outside. If it was on the inside, we could never have seen it. We're stuck on the outside.

There's a sort of shed a little off to the left of the main entrance. I think it might have been intended as a place to park bikes, by someone who didn't realize very few people ride their bike to church. So it has become the setting for a life-sized manger.

The first time they set it up was our second Christmas here. We were both feeling rather blue, missing our families and not yet come to terms with our status as ghosts, and the fuss of setting everything up and working out the kinks turned out to be exactly the kind of distraction we needed.

Joseph and Maria have been here since that first year, obviously, as has the baby Jesus, one sheep, and one of the wise men. I've never been quite clear on which wise man is which—and neither have the people setting it up because the same mannequin never brings the same gift or wears the same clothes two years in a row—but there wasn't enough money to bring them all the first year. The two colleagues showed up three years later, bringing lots of pretty and sparkling gifts.

Better late than never.

I say Jesus has been here from the start, but the one currently waiting to make his grand entrance on Christmas Eve is actually the fifteenth doll playing the part. It's worrisome how popular it is to steal the baby Jesus. I don't think I want to know what happens to them once they leave sacred ground.

The animals have also slowly trickled in over the years. One sheep became five, soon joined by a donkey and a cow. We only have the head of the cow because making the whole thing would be too costly and take up too much space but all the others are the right size and with the correct number of limbs.

Clothilde and I have been known to spend an evening or two inside the manger, sitting next to the wise men or pretending to ride the donkey, feeling a little less lonely for a few blessed hours.

Once the manger is in place, it's the church's turn. Most of the decorations are set up on the inside, so we never see them, but the porch is usually hung with holly and other twigs and greenery, and live lights are set up along the main path from the parking lot to the church entrance for Mass. On Christmas Eve, more than a hundred lights are lit up all across the cemetery.

It's my favorite moment of the year.

Even though our families aren't here and the people setting out the lights never knew us, it makes us feel remembered.

Tonight is December twenty-third and we're spending the evening in the manger. Outside, it's raining and a nasty western wind is starting up, and even though we can't feel the cold or the wind on our ghostly bodies, we can feel the misery. I've opted to sprawl out on the donkey's hay, with my back against the west wall and my legs crossed at my ankles, while Clothilde is perching on the crib. She usually prefers higher ground but the only other option is on the donkey and she doesn't like that for some reason. As usual, her legs swing back and forth, passing through the wood of the crib on every swing.

"I'm telling you, that's Balthazar," Clothilde says, eying the mannequin wearing the blue robes and offering a gilded box to the empty crib where the baby Jesus will lie. The box is empty—we checked—but I *think* it's supposed to contain spices of some sort. Unfortunately, I didn't really pay attention to the details of the story of Jesus' birth while I was alive, and access to research materials is woefully slim in a cemetery.

"You're just saying that because it's the only wise man name you know." I eye the box and wonder if I'd even be able to differentiate one spice from another if I still had taste buds. I know I loved cinnamon and clover—but even the memory of their smell eludes me.

Clothilde shrugs. We share a silence—another thing we've become experts at—while Clothilde frowns out at the dreary night. "I wish we'd get a white Christmas for once. Southern France sucks at helping with the spirit of things."

"The last time we had snow for Christmas around here was in 1962," I say. "I was nine." I sigh happily. "It was the most magical night of my life. I made a snowman! Stole a carrot from Maman for the nose and everything."

Clothilde huffs. "I wasn't even born yet. Why couldn't we be buried in the Massif Central or something? I'm sure those guys have snow every Christmas."

The natural answer to that question is, of course, that you don't choose where you're buried based on where there will be snow for the holidays. Your family choose for you, so they can come visit. Except in our cases, we never get any visits. Our families either don't care or don't know where we are.

Neither option is very uplifting.

We fall back into silence. I listen to the drip of rain on the manger's tin roof and the wind rustling the branches of the nearby trees. No other sounds come from the village, not even a car. Everybody is sensibly at home, preparing for tomorrow's big feast.

Until a car pulls into the parking lot, the light of its headlights pouring through the main gate, lighting up the nearest gravestones.

I exchange a glance with Clothilde. It must be almost midnight. Who'd come here at this time of night and in such weather?

Clothilde jumps out in the rain to get a look. The rain falls right through her—the reason we prefer to stay out of the rain because it's such a stark reminder we're no longer corporeal. "It's the hearse. They're bringing someone in."

A funeral the day before Christmas? That's bound to put a damper on the holiday spirit.

Rain be damned, we approach the gate to greet the newcomer. Not a large percentage of dead people become ghosts, so chances are this isn't a new arrival, but we like to accompany the casket through the cemetery anyway. Especially on nights like these.

Two men pull the white casket onto the transportation stretcher and gently roll it toward the church's side entrance. We follow close behind.

"No wreaths," Clothilde comments.

"Maybe they'll come later. They don't always come with the casket."

"*Some* always come with the casket."

I sidestep a puddle even though I can't get my feet wet. Clothilde steps right through it. I like to pretend, she doesn't care.

"The funeral must be tomorrow morning or they wouldn't bring the casket in now," I say. "There's no way they'll be holding the Midnight Mass with a casket up front and center."

Clothilde scoffs. "That sounds like a fun funeral, with the casket surrounded by pretty Christmas decorations and reminders of the party the deceased is missing out on."

It does sound like the perfect way to ruin Christmas for this poor soul's loved ones. For years to come.

One of the men releases the stretcher and goes to unlock the door. "Guess we'll see tomorrow if we have a new ghost," Clothilde says, eying the casket. "Wanna make a bet?"

Ghosts only wake up after the service. Betting on whether or not the dead person has unfinished business and will join us as a ghost is one of Clothilde's favorite pastimes. We have no worldly goods to bet and no possible stakes. Still, it was fun to play for a while. Until I realized Clothilde always won.

"I'm good," I tell her. "Why don't you make your prognostic?"

The two men start pushing the stretcher through the door.

"Nah, I don't think—"

A polite knock sounds from the casket. "Hello?" a gentle male voice says from inside the casket. "Can anybody hear me? I appear to be locked in."

The door closes behind the stretcher and it's just me and a shocked Clothilde in the rain.

Seems like, for once, I should have taken the bet.

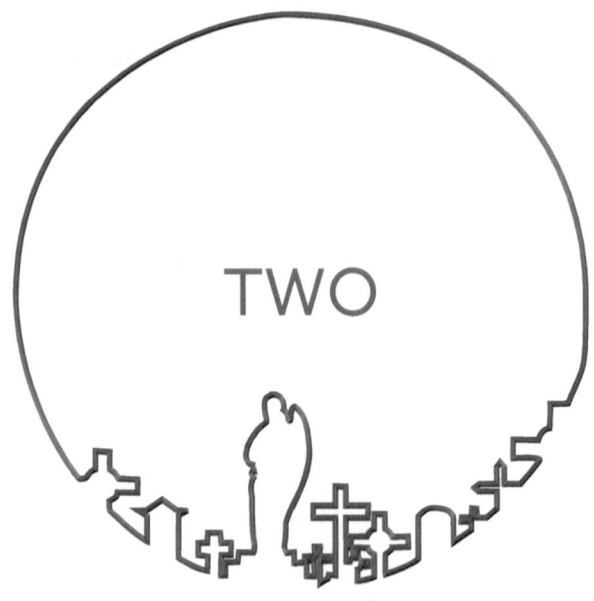

TWO

When the casket exits the church the next day, we're ready for him. Clothilde perches on the staircase railing while I lean against the church wall next to the main entrance. The rain stopped around four in the morning and by the time the sun came up, the sky was a clear blue we don't often see around here in winter, and the temperature must have dropped below zero judging by the state of the rare tufts of grass around some of the less maintained graves. As noon is approaching, a couple of clouds are gathering overhead and more forming in the west. It still qualifies as a beautiful day.

"There are, like, five people max attending the service," Clothilde says. "And I haven't seen any wreaths." Her tone is nonchalant, that of a teenager who doesn't care one way or another. I know it's just posturing, though. Clothilde cares, a lot. And if there's one thing she doesn't like, it's funerals with no loved ones to accompany the deceased to their final resting place.

The fact she probably wasn't accompanied to her own grave *might* have something to do with it.

"We'll see soon enough," I say. They sounded the bells less than five minutes ago, signaling the end of the service. "Do you think he'll come out of the casket straight away?" I ask. I need to distract my friend, but I'm also genuinely curious. "Nobody's ever woken up *before* the service, have they?"

Clothilde shakes her head. "We also usually get screaming and not polite knocking when they wake up."

Yeah, waking up inside a sealed casket? Not fun. Personally, I screamed for days. Don't ask me how it works, but the casket only releases us when we accept we're ghosts. So the duration depends on the person.

The church doors slide open on a creak. I assume a gust of air escapes because a couple of dead leaves blow down the stairs. I can't feel a thing. I straighten and Clothilde jumps down from her perch.

"Hello?" a faint voice says.

Clothilde meets my gaze, baffled. "He's still awake, and still *polite*. How is that even possible?"

I shrug. "I panic when in small spaces. Don't ask me to explain this weird behavior. By all accounts, he should be screaming his head off."

The casket on its stretcher is carried down to the path by six men. One is the priest, and three are cemetery workers we see here regularly. Only two faces are new: a young man in his early twenties with a bright red beanie and a worn bomber jacket, and a woman in her forties with long, salt-and-pepper hair and round, gold-rimmed glasses making her bright blue eyes look perpetually surprised and curious.

"Hello?" the new ghost says again. "Can anybody hear me? I'm not very fond of the dark...."

"Not very fond of—" Clothilde throws her hands in the air. "Nobody is this calm about being dead! That's not human!"

A head pops out of the casket.

Clothilde screams and I skid backward, a hand to my heart even though it hasn't been beating in thirty years.

Without great surprise, Clothilde uses offense as the best defense. "You can't come out of the casket *before* you're buried! You're supposed to crawl out of the ground. Through the dirt. The horror of being buried alive! You can't just *sit* there and say hello like you're a receptionist at a dentist's office."

"Oh." The man turns this way and that, taking in the cemetery and the church. I'd say he's in his mid-fifties, with a huge mop of gray hair and bushy eyebrows. His face is gaunt but there's a kind twist to his mouth and his dark eyes seem to be the keepers of marvelous secrets. I half expect him to invite us into his lap so he can tell us a story.

He's sitting up *through* the casket's lid as if he's in a canoe. Gnarly hands grip the edge—which is a surprise in itself; ghosts usually need some time to learn how to go through some things and on top of others—as he follows the gentle movements of the stretcher toward his final resting place.

"Is this where they're burying me? I must say, it doesn't look so bad." He turns to study me where I'm stumbling along next to the woman with the salt-and-pepper hair, and looks me up and down, taking in my ghostly appearance and the fact I'm walking through gravestones. "Say, Monsieur, would you say this is a decent cemetery to spend eternity in?"

"I, uh…" What am I supposed to answer? "I don't really have much to compare it to." Most people in their thirties don't spend much time in cemeteries—unless they die. In which case you're stuck with the one.

"Yes, of course." He nods to himself before turning to Clothilde.

Clothilde is also keeping pace with the tiny funeral procession, but from a greater distance. I think she's curious—who wouldn't be?—but her expression shows nothing but suspicion. When the man turns toward her, her eyes narrow.

"Delighted to make your acquaintance, Mademoiselle," he says genially. "Théophile Clément, at your service."

Clothilde's expression is nothing short of hilarious. Politeness is not the way to impress girls like her. If she'd still been alive, Clothilde would have been fifty. Clearly, our minds don't age any more than our bodies do once we become ghosts—and doing "old people stuff" is the best way to be ignored by the resident teenager.

Not wanting Clothilde to insult our new friend before he's even out of his casket, I jump in. "That's Clothilde, and I'm Robert. We're the only ghosts in this cemetery at the moment. Tell me, have you been awake for long?"

"Well." Théophile takes another look around, this time taking in the position of the sun and the bare trees of the forest on the north side of the cemetery. "It was Wednesday the last time I went to bed. When I woke up, it was dark and I was in here." He tries to knock on the casket lid, but it turns out to be beyond his capabilities and his hand goes right through. "It's rather difficult to tell time in such places."

"So you couldn't pop your head out until just now?" Clothilde asks. Curiosity is getting the better of her, I'm glad to see.

"I can't say that I tried." Théophile moves his hands through the lid, through the side of the casket, holding on to the rim. "I did an awful lot of knocking but I'm beginning to see this doesn't mean much." He tries knocking from the inside. His hand goes straight though. "Huh. It may appear the casket has only recently opened."

Even with years of practice, Clothilde and I can't knock on anything either. We can make it look like we're knocking, but there is never any sound, be it for the dead or the living. The only time a ghost can make a sound—and it's only audible to other ghosts—is when they're stuck inside the casket. I guess even Théophile had to follow that rule.

The stretcher comes to a stop in front of a newly dug grave. The gravediggers came two days ago, so we knew there would be a burial soon, but we weren't expecting it to happen on Christmas Eve. The three cemetery workers help set up the casket, then leave. The priest stands in his usual spot at the head of the grave, while the woman and young man stand at the foot. Given the distance they keep between them, I assume they're not very close.

Théophile observes all this from his perch in the casket. When the priest starts talking, he leans toward me and whispers, "Do you think I should come out now?"

I hold back my laugh. "You might as well. I've never seen anyone halfway out of their casket when it was covered in dirt before. It might not be the best first experience as a ghost."

"Quite." With great care, he stands up, to display he's wearing a classy but worn two-piece suit, the first two buttons of his white shirt open. He hesitates before stepping out, testing the solidity of the casket.

"You can't affect the physical world anymore, old man," Clothilde says. She's found a perching spot on the Gerard family grave in the neighboring plot. "Nor can it affect you. You can walk on air if you want."

Eying the gap between his casket and the solid earth, Théophile doesn't seem convinced. He very carefully takes a long step, going over the side of his casket instead of simply passing through, and finds himself two steps away from the priest—who seems to be doing his usual spiel for the people he knows nothing about.

"Your family couldn't tell the priest anything about you to make this more personal?" I ask.

"My family?" Théophile is brushing down his suit, convincingly enough that ghostly dust particles fall from his trousers.

I point to the woman and young man at the foot of the grave, both staring intently at the casket. No tears, but that's fairly common, all things considered. Not everybody likes to let out all their emotions when out in public.

Théophile's bushy eyebrows draw together. "I've never seen these people before in my life. Why would you make such an assumption?"

THREE

THERE'S NOTHING LIKE a good mystery to get Clothilde engaged. The minute Théophile tells us he doesn't know his two mourners, she jumps down from her perch and approaches the pair.

She starts with the young man in the red beanie. He stands half a head taller than Clothilde, his hands deep in the pockets of his bomber jacket. Tufts of dirty blond hair curl around the beanie in the back and his deep-set brown eyes stay fixated on Théophile's casket. I don't think he's listening to a word the priest says but I'm willing to bet he's taken note of every single movement the long-haired lady to his left makes.

There's a tension between the two, like either could explode into action at the slightest provocation. I first thought they were members of the same family who had some history.

"I don't think he's had a decent shower in a while," Clothilde comments. "We should probably be glad we don't have a sense of smell, judging by the layer of dirt and grease on his neck."

Beanie-boy must be more sensitive to ghostly activity than most. He lifts a hand to scrub at his neck while he shifts his weight to the other foot.

"Bad teeth, skin that hasn't seen sunblock in years but lots of sun, all of his clothing has seen better days." Clothilde meets my gaze. "I think he might be homeless."

She moves over to the lady. "Doesn't bother coloring her hair to hide the gray. The dress and coat are understated but clean and probably expensive. Those glasses are *gleaming*. It's not possible to have glasses made of actual gold, is it?"

Instead of joining in on the research, Théophile is exploring his new home. Reading the inscriptions on the nearest graves, poking at the plastic flowers on the Gerard plot, gazing beyond the cemetery walls in search of who knows what. When Clothilde mentions golden glasses, he snaps to attention. "Gold is far too heavy for such use. It would be horribly heavy on nose and ears alike."

"Good to know," Clothilde grumbles. Eyes narrowed, she brings her hands to her hips. "If you don't know these two, you might want to help investigate before they leave. Chances are, they're your ticket out of here."

"Ticket out?" Théophile's head whips from one side to the other. Is he looking for a train?

"Only people with unfinished business linger as ghosts," I tell him. With his odd arrival, I haven't even gotten around to doing my usual spiel. "Clothilde and I usually help. Either by figuring out what the unfinished business is, or by finishing it."

"Unfinished business." He says it as if he's trying on the words to see how they taste. "Hah! Hardly surprising I'm there, then. I take it you two would also need decades to tie up everything?"

No, we're still here because we'd need to leave the cemetery to finish our business. Oddly enough, the people who killed us have never come to visit.

Clothilde sneers at Théophile but luckily keeps her thoughts to herself.

"You have a lot of unfinished business, I take it?" I step aside to let the priest access the lift that will lower the casket into the hole without stepping through me. He wouldn't notice—we've met him often enough to know he has no sensibility to ghosts whatsoever—but I hate it.

Théophile goes down on all fours to study the mechanism of the lift. He still hasn't spared his mourners a single look. "I make it a point of honor never to finish anything," he says. "Never saw the point in following other people's orders or bending to their wishes. When I'm done with something, I don't linger. Take high school, for example." He jumps back up and addresses Clothilde directly, for some reason—does he assume she should still be in high school? This won't end well. "Why should I learn by heart the years of such and such battle a random historian has decided were more important than other dates? Why should *they* decide the information to be stored in my brain? I listened to the parts

I found interesting and left to do more interesting things when the testing started."

I groan inwardly. I *really* hope this guy will figure out his unfinished business quickly, because I do not want to spend years and years with him here. Clothilde and I get on each other's nerves sometimes, sure, and bored out of our minds quite often. But we're also best friends and we have a routine. I don't want Théophile to mess that up.

So when Clothilde's temper predictably flares and she stalks away from the two mourners to follow up on Théophile's comments, I take her place. Logically, the answer to our prayers should be with these two. If I could only get them to talk.

Before I can even decide on a line of attack, the woman with the golden glasses turns slightly and gives the young man a once-over. Although the two have clearly been acutely aware of each other throughout the ceremony, this is the first time either has looked at the other.

The man in the red beanie's eyes twitch in her direction but turn back to the lowering casket before their reach their destination.

"She looks like a nice lady," I say to him. "It might be a good idea to talk to her. Figure out what her link to Théophile is."

Live people can't hear us, but the ones who are sensitive to otherworldly activities can somehow absorb what we say to them anyway. I think their subconscious can hear us and brings our words up as ideas to their own minds. Unfortunately, it's not an exact science, but we make do. It's the only way we have of solving dead people's mysteries around here.

The young man's sensitivity is confirmed when he turns to

face the woman. "I'm Xavier," he says in a rough voice. "You knew him?" He nods toward the grave.

The casket is at the bottom and the priest has thrown in his handful of dirt. It seems neither of the mourners have the intention of doing the same and the priest is awkwardly rounding things up so he can leave and get ready for the Midnight Mass. Clothilde is listening to Théophile talk and the way her eyebrows are reaching for the sky is not promising.

The woman's face flickers with what I think is disappointment. "I'm Mathilda," she says and holds out a hand. "And yes, I had the misfortune of knowing Théophile."

Xavier lets out something between a huff and a sigh as he reluctantly shakes her hand after wiping it off on his pants. "I take it I'm not the only one he disappointed in life?"

Clothilde comes stomping to join us, while Théophile seems to be aiming for the nativity scene. The spring in his step is nothing short of joyous. Is it possible to be happy to be dead?

"The guy takes *pride* in disappointing people," she almost growls. "If anyone ever shows the slightest indication of expecting anything from him, he's out. Nobody but Théophile dictates what Théophile does."

I acknowledge what she says with a nod but don't make a reply. I want to hear what Mathilda has to say to Xavier.

"Théophile leaves a *long* trail of disappointed people behind him." There's compassion for the young man in her tone but also a hardness that I'm guessing is especially fitting when talking about our newest ghost. "You shouldn't feel bad about it; it has nothing to do with you personally."

Xavier doesn't look like he believes her, but he keeps silent and burrows deeper into the collar of his jacket. More clouds have blown in during the burial and the lack of sun is probably felt keenly by those who still have corporeal bodies.

"Besides," Mathilda continues, "I'm guessing you're here because you got something from his estate? Nobody else would even know about the funeral."

I'm starting to understand the lack of wreaths and mourners.

Xavier nods. "I've apparently inherited a house." He doesn't seem to quite believe his own words. "Nothing is done according to the current norms because he didn't believe in following rules, but it's still a house. A nice one." His voice cracks on the last words.

"Indeed it is." Mathilda reaches out to pull on Xavier's elbow and the pair walks slowly toward the parking lot. Neither spares as much as a glance at the grave. Clothilde and I trail behind, listening in. "If you got the house, I assume it's because of the law and not something Théophile did?"

A curt nod.

Mathilda pushes her glasses up her nose. "Me, I officially got the half of my business that Théophile still owned. I've managed everything for ten years and he never helped or bothered me, so it won't actually change much. But it's nice to know it's all officially mine."

"We can't let them leave without figuring out what that jerk's unfinished business is," Clothilde says as we approach the gate. Ghosts can't go past that barrier.

"It seems unfinished business is what he does," I reply. "But if it doesn't bother *him*, why would it be keeping him here? There has to be something—hopefully *one* thing—that's unfinished even in his mind."

Two steps from the gate, the young Xavier stops. His gaze is distant and his breath is short. "He's the reason my life is so miserable," he says to his feet. "It's because of him my mom overworked herself so much she didn't realize she had cancer before it was too late. He starts something, gets everybody around him excited to go with him, then drops everything and leaves. At the worst possible time." His anger is taking over, his voice rising and his posture becoming less cowed.

Mathilda nods in understanding and patiently waits for the rest.

"He left two days after I was born," Xavier spits out. "When the hospital staff told him it was his job to do the paperwork to officially name me. Add in my mom expecting him to keep their business afloat for a month and he was gone.

"The jerk was my dad."

FOUR

We watch as the taillights of Mathilda's car disappear down the road. Xavier was on foot but accepted her offer of a ride to his new home. According to the clock on the church it's mid-afternoon, but it's almost dark already. There's not a speck of blue sky in sight, only heavy, dark clouds. It looks like we're getting a wet and depressing Christmas.

In the company of the most selfish ghost I've ever encountered.

"Having a kid should be important to anyone, right?" Clothilde says. "Even self-centered liars?"

I look toward the church and spot Théophile in the manger, apparently studying the craftsmanship of the cow. "I certainly hope so," I reply on a sigh. "At least it gives us an angle of attack. Except, if his business *is* with his son, I have no idea how we're going to resolve it. I doubt that man is ever coming back here."

Her jaw jutting out with hardened resolve, Clothilde marches toward Théophile like a general going to war. "The issue will be resolved in *his* head. And we're going to figure out how. I'm *not* spending eternity with that loser."

When we reach him, Théophile is riding the donkey, a joyful smile on his face. "It's a shame I can't feel the fur. It looks wonderfully soft."

"You lied to us." Clothilde crosses her arms and widens her stance. If she hadn't been wearing her usual ankle-length jeans and flowing white blouse, she'd look downright intimidating. "You said you didn't know either of your mourners."

By the way his nose tips up and his hands smooth down his vest, I can tell he's going to deny it. Which I don't have the patience for today, so I speak before he can. "The woman was a business associate of yours. It's kind of hard to forget someone you work closely with."

Théophile sniffs. He seems to be about to deny everything, gets a look at Clothilde's furious face, and deflates. "Fine. I knew Mathilda. But I don't see why she'd show up to my funeral. There was no love lost between us. The young man, I've never seen before, though."

"You left him and his mother when he was two days old," I say. "I suppose it's reasonable to assume he's changed since then. Especially since he appears to have been homeless for some time."

That does the trick. Théophile forgets he was sitting on the donkey and is suddenly standing a foot off the ground, halfway through the stuffed animal. He's been quite adept at being a ghost this far, but everyone has their limits.

"That was David?" he asks. His voice is almost uncertain.

"Oh, God, you have even more kids you've run out on?" Clothilde throws her hands in the air and pretends to choke Théophile from afar.

Théophile straightens, and when he realizes he's floating mid-air, drops to the ground. His nose is in the air again. "I have not 'run out on' more than one boy, I assure you. Just the one, about twenty years ago. And his name was David."

"Except you refused to do the paperwork to name him," I say. "And I'm guessing the mom decided *she* wanted to decide the name, since she was the one who had to do everything after you left. His name is Xavier."

"Xavier! But that's— Oh. Well, then." He crosses his arms only to uncross them immediately.

"Would we be right to assume your unfinished business is with your son?" I ask.

"Why would it be about him? I've always made a point of never finishing anything."

"Yes, so we've understood." I glance at the mannequins of Mary and Joseph, already set up so they hover over the empty crib where Jesus will appear tonight. Without the baby, they look kind of sad, like they're happy about a pile of hay while ignoring everybody else around them. Once the baby is in place, though, they'll be equal parts happy and worried parents. Like I imagine most parents feel when they look down on their newborn for the first time.

"Still. Leaving your son behind can't sit entirely right, even with someone used to disappointing everyone around him?"

Théophile huffs. "I don't understand why he was here at all."

"Clearly, the mother did *her* work well, and listed you as the father. The boy just inherited your house, and probably most of your belongings."

The shock of this news is so strong that Théophile's ghostly form flickers. I have a second to hope it means he's moving on, but then he comes back.

Clothilde cackles. "Shocked the state helps you take care of your kid, Théophile? It's very hard to leave your children with nothing in France. And if you don't have a will, they get everything. A case where doing nothing actually is doing something."

That shuts him up. I'm not sure if he needs time to reflect on his life and his choices or if he's avoiding us, but he spends the rest of the afternoon walking the cemetery, discovering his limitations as a ghost. Clothilde and I stay in the manger, chatting about the wise men and their gifts. Maybe we could drop a hint with one of the ladies who set it up for them to properly label the gifts? Twenty years of asking ourselves the same questions get a bit tedious.

When the bells strike nine thirty, people start filing in. Some come by car, quite a few on foot. Most families will start their Christmas feast once they get home, but the ones with very young children have probably already dug into the foie gras. I remember the taste well enough to know I miss it.

We stay in the manger, Clothilde perched on the donkey and me sitting on the floor next to Joseph. This way, when the churchgoers come to check out the nativity scene, it almost feels like they're talking to and seeing us.

Every year, I study every single person passing through the church doors. I know we're not far from the village where I grew up and where part of my family presumably still lives, and I cling to the faint possibility they would come here for Midnight Mass one year. If they do, I don't want to miss it.

This is probably why my first reaction to seeing Xavier and Mathilda show up again is jealousy.

Théophile spent his entire life running from everything—and yet they come back for him.

"Théophile!" I yell into the night. "You have visitors!" An old couple by the stairs startle, and after a shared look, hurry inside the church.

Théophile appears and when he sees his son, goes straight to him. The pair has stopped some distance off, apparently arguing whether or not to attend Mass. Although I frankly don't want to, I saunter over to join them. This *is* our best chance at getting rid of Théophile.

"We've already listened to the priest's yapping once today," Xavier says on a sigh. "Isn't that enough?"

"It's Christmas and you're going home to a feast of buttered pasta for one," Mathilda says with a kind smile. "You can afford to listen to the words of a kind man for an hour or two."

"There's a box of foie gras somewhere in the basement, if you can find it," Théophile says to his son. His voice is distant and the way he's looking at Xavier is very intense. I think he might be trying to see himself in the young man.

"Maybe I'll have a look around in the basement," Xavier says. "See if the old man had any treats hidden away."

Théophile whips around to stare at me.

"Your son is sensitive to ghosts," I tell him. "If you have something to say to him, he might even hear it." As if the man is ready for something as decent as an apology.

"Hey, look," Mathilda says, and points to the sky. "I think it's snowing."

At first I think she's simply trying to get Xavier to think of something else, until a snowflake lands on the young man's nose and promptly melts.

Clothilde appears at my side, her face even more youthful than usual. "It's snowing? For Christmas? Really?"

I can't help but laugh. "Looks like it. Go enjoy your first white Christmas, Clothilde."

On a happy laugh, Clothilde does just that.

Xavier seems equally happy. He tips his head to the sky and closes his eyes, letting the snow fall on his face. "And I'll have a warm bed and a roof over my head tonight," he whispers.

Théophile is the only one in the group who doesn't care about the snow. He's so close to his son's face, it borders on creepy. It's a good thing only us ghosts can see him. "That's not right," he says. "How can a son of mine fall so low he doesn't even have a roof over his head?"

"Maybe he didn't inherit your lack of empathy and sense of community," I say.

Théophile falls silent but doesn't stop his fierce scrutiny of his son. Around us, people are exclaiming about the snow, some happy, some worried about getting home after Mass.

"I didn't know how to be a father," Théophile says. His eyes are still on his son, but I think he's talking to me. "He was better off without me. I would have messed him up, like I do everything. It's no great issue when you mess up a business deal or a friendship. But a fragile, little life? I panicked." He reaches out to touch his son's cheek, but lacking practice, he goes right through. "I did what I thought was best for you, Dav—Xavier. Really."

The young man definitely hears his father. He turns to gaze toward the newly dug grave across the cemetery. "I guess I should thank my father for the house," he says. "He hasn't done anything for me while he was alive, but at least dead, thanks to him, I'll be warm tonight."

Mathilda sighs and gives him a hug. "If I needed proof you're his son, that kind of whacked-out logic will do it. But yes, let's look at the positive side. You have a warm place to sleep tonight, and every other night this winter, and we get snow for Christmas!"

The pair walk into the church and soon, the doors shut behind the last of the revelers. Outside, in the snow but leaving no footprints, stand three ghosts. And let's not forget the mannequins of the nativity scene.

"Seems you managed to help your son, after all," I say to Théophile, who appears to be frozen in place as he stares at the spot where his son disappeared into the church. "Better late than never?"

His confused eyes meet mine. "I helped him?" There's definitely hope in his tone.

"I'd say so. Giving a home to a homeless person definitely qualifies as helping."

"Huh." His eyes go back to the church doors and as a huge smile grows on his face, his body becomes more and more transparent.

I open my mouth to tell him goodbye, or to point out he's finished his business, but in the end I stay silent. I don't want to interrupt the obvious happiness he's feeling. I hope he gets to take it with him wherever he's going next. Despite having been a rather despicable human being, he must also have been very lonely. Finishing off knowing he helped his son feels right.

Five minutes later, an excited Clothilde comes back. "Where'd the jerk go?"

"He moved on."

"Really? That was quick." There's a slight hint of envy in her tone, but I know it won't linger. We're used to being just the two of us and can take years more while we wait our turn.

I'm just glad we don't have to wait with Théophile.

One of the church ladies slips out the side door with a bundle in her arms.

"Ah, here comes the baby Jesus."

So we hold up our own Christmas tradition. We sit with Mary and Joseph as their baby is "born" and watch our cemetery being quietly covered in a blanket of snow with the congregation singing Christmas carols inside the church.

"I've always wanted a white Christmas," Clothilde says happily as she gives the Jesus doll a pat.

See? No need for fancy gifts to have a perfect Christmas.

Also by R.W. Wallace

Mystery

Ghost Detective Novels
Beyond the Grave
Unveiling the Past
Beneath the Surface
Piercing the Veil

Ghost Detective Shorts
Just Desserts
Lost Friends
Family Bonds
Common Ground
Till Death
Family History
Heritage
New Beginnings
Far From Home
Severed Ties
Eternal Bond
Harsh Expectations
Dull Expectations

Ghost Detective Collections
Unfinished Business, Vol 1

The Tolosa Mystery Series
The Red Brick Haze
The Red Brick Cellars
The Red Brick Basilica

SHORT STORY COLLECTIONS
Deep Dark Secrets
A Thief in the Night

ROMANCE

FRENCH OFFICE ROMANCE SERIES
Flirting in Plain Sight
Hiding in Plain Sight

STANDALONE NOVELS
Love at First Flight

HOLIDAY STORIES

COLLECTIONS
Heartwarming Holiday Tales

SHORT STORIES
The Case of the Disappearing Gingerbread City
Crooks and Nannies

YOUNG ADULT SHORT STORY COLLECTIONS
Tales From the Trenches

Find all R.W. Wallace's books:

rwwallace.com/allbooks

ABOUT THE AUTHOR

R.W. Wallace writes in most genres, though she tends to end up in mystery more often than not. Dead bodies keep popping up all over the place whenever she sits down in front of her keyboard.

The stories mostly take place in Norway or France; the country she was born in and the one that has been her home for two decades. Don't ask her why she writes in English—she won't have a sensible answer for you.

Her Ghost Detective short story series appears in *Pulphouse Magazine*, starting in issue #9.

You can find all her books, long and short, all genres, on rwwallace.com.

www.ingramcontent.com/pod-product-compliance
Lightning Source LLC
LaVergne TN
LVHW041716060526
838201LV00043B/775